IN THE MIDST OF IT ALL

Sandra J. Harden

IN THE MIDST OF IT ALL

WRITTEN BY:

SANDRA J. HARDEN

FOREWORD BY: PASTOR JAMES HARDEN

ISBN: 978-1-7364457-4-7 (Paperback)
978-1-7364457-5-4 (E-book)

Library of Congress Control Number: 2021905948

Book Cover Design by: Prize Publishing House

Printed by: Prize Publishing House, LLC
in the United States of America.

First printing edition 2021.

Prize Publishing House
P.O. Box 9856
Chesapeake, VA 23321

www.PrizePublishingHouse.com

DEDICATION

I dedicate this book to honor my grandmother, Viola Polk, who taught me the greatest thing in the world: love and look to the hills from whence cometh my help.

To my husband, Pastor James R. Harden, for believing in my vision.

To my son, RyJaeh, who pushed me to press my way to do anything I put my mind to.

To my mother, Barbara, for birthing me to be the woman I am today.

FOREWORD

Follow my example as I follow the examples of Christ. – 1 Corinthians 11:1

I have never been more honored than I am at this moment to be able to write this for my beautiful wife. When my wife, First Lady Sandra Harden, asked me to write this foreword for her, I was truly happy to do it. I have such high respect for this woman of God because she has shown such integrity and standards in life. I am overjoyed to lend my thoughts, time, and solemn words to such a great project.

As I watched her time after time get out of the bed and put her thoughts to paper, I began to think about the conversations and the laughter that we have shared throughout our time together. As I continue to think and sit here, I start to reminisce over the fact that words cannot express the unworthiness I feel to be writing the foreword for this great mother, mentor, counselor, and friend. Just know the author of this great manuscript has truly laid and labored before God to share and impart into the millions of people that will read this great manuscript entitled, *In the Midst of It All.* There are no words to describe the power and healing virtue to be revealed in the pages of this book. It will mentally, emotionally, and spiritually inspire you and all who read it. It is truly going to captivate your heart and mind. Get ready for *In the Midst of It All!!!*

In Christ Jesus.

-Pastor James Harden

CONTENTS

INTRODUCTION

Have you ever sat in a quiet place and talked to yourself out loud? "Where do I go from here? How did I allow myself to get so low and so depressed? How could I have done things so differently? My life is a total mess and, the road I am traveling, I don't know how to fix it."

This point in my life is very scary. I knew I needed to remove myself from toxic people. I was repeating the cycle over and over. The more I tried to get out, the deeper I got into this situation. "Who can I turn to for help?"

The irony of this title is that in the midst of it all, I choose joy. When you see someone in the midst of all kinds of things, your faith is tested and tried. I had to remember the scripture Psalm 30:5, "Weeping may endure for a night, but joy comes in the morning." I kept knocking on doors that needed to be closed. I had to gain confidence in myself and have the assurance that I can make it. It is not because of anything that I have done, but because of God's grace and how He loves me in spite of. God will be with you through it all. God fights the battles even when you do not have the strength to fight.

Finally, I am thankful that the Lord was there to keep me. In the midst of it all, there is nothing too hard for God.

LOOKING FOR LOVE IN ALL THE WRONG PLACES

I grew up in a single-parent home. I always knew who my dad was, but he did not live in the same house, so I lacked a father figure. I lacked the little girl who wanted her daddy nearby to call her princess, so I grew up trying to find love in relationships. I thought because a guy called me pretty, he loved me. No, he used me.

Experiencing one relationship after another, I finally found the one to love me, so I married him because of the love. I was deeply in love listening to my grandmother talk about marriage. I was so excited to be a wife. I just knew it would work. I was wrong. He began to cheat. I thought I had lost my mind. "How can this happen to me when I have bragged to my friends how much in love I was?" I was a hot mess at this point. I thought I had lost my mind, but his cheating taught me the true love I desired.

In the midst of the hurt, I had to watch my husband and a child with another woman. This was the worst thing I ever had to endure. I was lost and wanted to die. After all I have done, this is happening to me. I felt as if I was suffering. I still had to face people.

Years later, we divorced. I was devastated because all I knew was hurt. What were happiness and joy, and how do I get it? I was raised in the church, attending Sunday School and Bible Study. My grandma kept me there, but I was still not thinking about being saved. I wanted to get past all the hurt. Every person I came in contact with hurt me, so my heart grew bitter, and I hated myself for being so stupid. I was struggling from day to day. I had to figure this out on my own – how to change to be a better person and stop men from giving me that sweet talk, and I fall for it every time. I deserved better, but how? I cried out. "I need help. Bring me back to the person I once knew."

I moved on, then here came the lustful eye and the sweet talk. Then came stupidity and life going to hell in a hand basket. I thought, "What kind of example am I setting for myself," but I turned to a married man for comfort because of hurt. Now, this was the biggest mistake of my life. It cost me my character. It cost my name to be destroyed. I lived with that for years. I had to get my life in order. I decided if I do not turn my life back into the hands of a man that I know will not hurt me, I will die from something, and it will not be pretty.

One Sunday morning, I got up, and I was determined to go to church. The preacher spoke the message, "I'm Not That Way Anymore," and the altar call was open to anyone that wanted to give their life to Christ. Come just as you are – wounded, hurt, sick, and in pain. I sat there. Everyone else was going, and I sat there. The preacher asked, "Is there one?" I found my legs shaking. I felt all the things I had done. I got up and made my way down to the altar and lifted my hands. I screamed and yelled for the Lord to save me. The preacher prayed, and I felt myself getting lighter. Burdens and weights were being lifted. After being saved that day, I still was not totally sold out for Jesus. I was a babe in Christ, but I was determined not to see the old life that I lived again.

IN THE MIDST OF IT ALL

It takes strength to stand alone. It takes strength to endure abuse, heartaches, and disappointment, but most of all, it takes courage to live. God uses obstacles to prepare us, test us, and train us to be better equipped to be a blessing to others.

There is always a blessing on the other side of the mountain. My faith was tested and tried many times, but I kept pushing. I began speaking into my spirit. I may have had the fire on me, but now I had the fire in me. I positioned myself to a comeback more remarkable than I have ever seen in my life.

I did not always choose the right path. In my life, I made plenty of mistakes. In a lot of situations, I jumped too soon. I have been down some hard roads and survived some very tough times. There were days I did not think I would make it. Nights that I cried all night long, dealing with physical, mental, and verbal abuse. Looking back over my life, I found my strength. I became the woman that would make a difference. I had to learn through these life experiences. There were a lot of twists and turns, but I made it through with prayer. I had to take a leap of faith, and I had to hold on to what I believed.

The abuse I suffered, I wanted to share the signs, but I did not know how. The question was, "Would anyone believe me?" I kept it to myself, never telling anyone. I was bound, loving a man that one day was sweet, and the next turned into someone I did not know. Hiding behind the bruises, I continued my daily activities, worn out from the worries of this world. By the grace of God, He kept me. I heard a small still voice speaking, "Before I allow you to die in the hands of a man, I will intervene on your behalf." It was so hard to walk away. Eventually, it got easier. I loved him even through the tears, but the abuse was unacceptable.

God released me. Still lonely at heart, I learned in the process to love myself. Although things looked a certain way, my state of mind needed to shift in the right direction. I had to use the strength that God gave me. I knew I needed to leap into another dimension, and that was faith. I was tired of being lost and stuck in the same me. It was time for me to get out of my comfort zone and spread my wings.

I did not want to talk about things that were happening in my life, so I kept a secret through my pain. The most important thing I decided to do was write my thoughts on paper and publish this book.

Emotionally drained, always wanting to fit in, I did much wrong in my life and finally have a chance to get it right, be heard, and share with others. It was time that I took care of myself. I was determined I was not going to let it get me down. After standing at the crossroads of many breakdowns, I knew the only person that could help me was me and God Himself.

After a lot of fasting and praying and after many tears, God hears and sees. I believe that when you pray and lift your burdens, He will fix them. I quoted my favorite scripture, Philippians 4:13. I realized in my wilderness experience that my testimony would be a blessing to the body of Christ when I came out. I wanted to stop looking at the trials I faced and focus on the woman I had become. I had to stop being stuck in the place I was for years.

How many roadblocks have stood in your path?

How many disappointments have you faced?

How long will a relationship last before true love appears?

How many mistakes have you made?

IN THE MIDST OF IT ALL

How many times have you been knocked down to your knees?

I had to go through some rough times. Some hard times to get to where I am now. It was not easy. That is when I decided I wanted to help to encourage anyone that life can be great if you learn to love yourself first. It takes strength to love. It takes determination and willingness to push.

Meditation Scriptures:

- ❖ 1 Peter 4:8
- ❖ Psalm 136:26
- ❖ 1 Corinthians 16:14
- ❖ Psalm 86:15

Dear Lord, walk with me every day. Fill me with Your blessings. Please help me on this path called life. May my days be filled with love and happiness. In Jesus' Name, Amen.

BE YOURSELF

Being yourself means you like who you are. Being yourself means living your life how you want to live it regardless of other people's opinions. Respect yourself. Do not worry about what others think; you cannot control them or their thoughts.

Live a happier life and do not get discouraged about the viewing of others. Always appreciate who you are and find a happy place in you that you love. Forgive yourself. Be honest with yourself about the way you feel and think. You have to train your mind to be stronger than your emotions. Be true to your principles. When you want to become a brand new you, you have to have self-love for yourself and everyone around you.

When someone says, "Be Yourself," you may ask what that means. They are giving words of encouragement and saying let others see the real you. Being yourself does not mean you have to walk alone. God will always be by your side. Be comfortable in your own shoes.

Psalm 139:14 tells us how we are wonderfully made. You must want to be better and learn from possible examples concerning yourself. God's word makes it plain that no one is perfect. Jesus, the perfect Lamb of the Most High, walked the earth to live and then die for your sins. God extends to you His unconditional love. Take time to be yourself. Take time to check your expectations of caring about what others think. Find your happiness in God.

IN THE MIDST OF IT ALL

The most important lesson I learned is you cannot count on someone to make you happy. God says love your inner self. You have the power to make a difference in your life. Take some alone time and embrace it.

When you are yourself, you will feel more strongly about yourself, and many will want to come into your presence.

Meditation Scriptures:

- ❖ Matthew 22:39
- ❖ Philippians 2:3
- ❖ Jeremiah 29:11
- ❖ Psalm 12:6-7
- ❖ Hebrews 3:13
- ❖ Luke 6:31

Lord, hear my prayers. I am coming to You with an open heart. I ask You to open the doors. I praise You and thank You. In Jesus' Name, Amen.

THE ODDS OF BEING DIFFERENT

Life can bring situations, and sometimes you think it's just not enough. You have to accept coming in first, second, or third place, and you ask yourself, "Why can't I be like everyone else?" In life, we do not follow the same timeline.

God is our judge, and you do not have to prove yourself to anyone. God set you apart so He can travel this journey with you. Dare to be different. No one needs to be the same. Have your own thoughts, dreams, and visions. God wants ordinary people to spread His word when it comes to telling others about Jesus. When I began to love the person inside me, I would look in the mirror and tell myself I am beautiful; I will be somebody, I am amazing, I will be what God has promised. Do not do what everyone else does and do what you are required to do. Everything you do will bring glory to God.

You may have different facial features, different hair color, different build but in the heart of God, you are fearfully and wonderfully made. You are God's greatest possession. You need to walk in your purpose. You are created to do great things.

How do you set yourself apart and stand out?

What do you do when you feel unworthy?

How can you change the way you think?

IN THE MIDST OF IT ALL

Meditation Scriptures:

- ❖ 1 Peter 2:9
- ❖ Jeremiah 1:5
- ❖ Romans 12:2
- ❖ Hebrews 12:1-3

God, I thank You for knowing me before I was formed on this earth. I humbly submit myself to You, Lord. You loved me even I did not love myself. In You, I put my trust. In Jesus' Name, Amen.

OUR PATH

God gave you this life, knowing you were strong enough to handle it. God may be the only one who knows how you feel daily. Continue to thank God for His unfailing love and being your protector, for giving you grace and mercy, and for guiding you when you did not know you needed it. Let go of past mistakes so God can take you where He wants you to go. Be still and wait on God. Even if it seems like a long time, wait.

You have the mind of Christ. Wherever you go and whatever you do, let your path be in Him. You want to be able to look back over your life and laugh. You had to learn lessons, but each lesson you went through has a blessing with your name on it. You want the courage to be able to walk, knowing that you pushed and made it.

Trust the plan over your life. Surrender it all over to God. It is not about having a lot; it is about trying to do your best. If you feel your best is not good enough, continue to push until you reach your destination. All of your hopes and dreams rest in God. Stay content until the Lord blesses your life. Let God fix your thoughts and thank Him for what He has done. God will carry you through to completion. Adhere to the Word of God and watch things come in divine order.

IN THE MIDST OF IT ALL

Meditation Scriptures:

- ❖ Matthew 6:8
- ❖ Isaiah 60:22
- ❖ Philippians 4:6-8
- ❖ Exodus 14:14

Dear Lord, show me the way. I have put everything today in Your hands. Carry my every burden. Cleanse me and fill me with Your peace. In Jesus' Name, Amen.

MAKE SOME NOISE

The reason you should have noise in your mouth is that in the midst of all you have been through and endured to the end, God still deserves the highest praise. He is a gracious, kind, loving, and forgiving savior. There is victory in the atmosphere for deliverance in your mouth. God will supply your needs according to what measure of faith you have. You must have that mustard seed faith. You must believe when you open your mouth that something has to change. It is time for you to sound it out. In this season, you must recognize that you could be everywhere and anywhere if it had not been for God's grace and mercy.

You must be a receiver of thanks. Mercy gives you the right to enter into His gates with thanksgiving, so you should not mind shouting to God for coming and rescuing you in your situation, helping you be a brand-new person, and helping you grow. You want to do things differently and get better results.

Do not let a day go by without making a joyful noise inside and out. When praises go up, blessings come down. When you make something, you cause it to exist. When you build praise, you cannot do things any kind of way. You cannot praise if you are unsure. You have to be confident in who God is. You have to perfect your praises. Have praise in your mouth. Give powerful praise because God is worthy of all praise. Break from being silent and make some noise. God has done some great things in your life. True worship focuses on our God. There is nothing in this world that is greater than making noise. Build your confidence, stay focused, and make some noise.

Meditation Scriptures:

- ❖ 1 Peter 1:13
- ❖ Psalm 100
- ❖ Galatians 6:12
- ❖ Colossians 3:16
- ❖ Philippians 4:8
- ❖ 2 Corinthians 10:5

Bless me, Lord. Thank You, Lord. Guide me, Lord. Forgive me, Lord. It is my prayer not to be anxious about anything. Lord, help me and teach me what to pray for. In Jesus' Name, Amen.

PRAYER

What is prayer? Communication between you and God. When you wake up, start your day with His name on your lips.

Jesus, I welcome this new day. It is Your gift to me. I thank You for Your grace of being alive. I thank You for Your refreshing and a chance for a new beginning by getting into a routine of chatting with You and being in Your presence.

Have a gentle conversation with Him like you are talking on the phone to a good friend or family. Pray at all times in the spirit with prayer and supplication. Sometimes we do not realize how much power there is in prayer. We must live victoriously; then, our prayer life has to be effective.

There are many forms of prayer: Praise, Supplication, Intercession, and Thanksgiving. The most incredible prayer to pray is The Lord's Prayer (Matthew 6:9-13). It brings peace to your life.

Meditation Scriptures:

- ❖ Philippians 4:6
- ❖ Psalm 102:17
- ❖ James 5:16
- ❖ Matthew 21:22

IN THE MIDST OF IT ALL

Lord, I pray that You hear my prayer. Touch me in a mighty way. I believe Your Word is true. I honor You. Lord, You are the great I am. In Jesus' Name, Amen.

STAY AWAKE

Sometimes you go out of your way for others, only to find out that you do not get the same as you have given. You find out that when you need them, they are nowhere to be found. The Bible says to have a renewed mind. You need to show compassion even when your friends and family treat you wrong.

You need to wake up. There will be a day when you will completely change the lives of others. You have to love one another despite your differences.

Sometimes you will feel hurt, confused, and upset, but letting this affect you will drain your energy. You have to be strong enough to go on. Even if the favor of helping them is not returned, stay in your lane. Never waste your time trying to please people.

There is a lesson to be learned about staying awake. Never forget who ignored you when you needed them. Just remember there will come a time when all of God's children will come together to have that loving heart, that giving spirit, and that loving smile.

Meditation Scriptures:

- ❖ Jeremiah 29:11
- ❖ 1 Peter 4:18

IN THE MIDST OF IT ALL

❖ Psalm 91
❖ Numbers 6:24-26

Lord, You are precious in my eyes, and I love You. I seek Your face. Teach me to stay awake. In Jesus' Name, Amen.

SISTAH TO SISTER

Be faithful in service. Be trustworthy. Love one another. You have to be your sister's keeper. You are responsible for their well-being. You are a gift from God. Some sisters spend a lot of time together. Some have disagreements and love from a distance. Pray daily for your sister, be an encouragement. When you see yourself the way God sees you, you can begin to see your fellow sister in Christ and love on them.

Proverbs 31:25 says that if you kneel before God, you can stand before anyone. God chose you out of all the people on earth to be His personal treasure. God loves you with a love that is increasing and overflowing. He has chosen you to be a blessing to many.

Sisters have to stick together. Hold each other up, do not be discouraged. Do not panic; hold on to God and trust God even when the circumstances have not changed. Trust His timing.

When you are having a bad day, a sister will stop what she is doing and call at the right time.

You need to rise up and become blessed. Sisters need greater visions so they can walk together spiritually. They should women of faith and encourage each other. When you cry, I shed a tear. When you hurt, I should feel your pain.

IN THE MIDST OF IT ALL

A spiritual mentor is essential. Romans 12 says do not pretend to love others, really love them. Sometimes you need someone who is willing to go above and beyond the call of duty. You need that sister that will talk about your situation instead of giving their opinion. Seek friends that know who God is and can pray for you.

You have to believe that you will overcome and be a part of someone's life. Sister, let me take your hand, and let's keep going forward, never in a hurry. We will rise together.

This year has been rough for many of us, but you are still here learning, growing, smiling, counting your many blessings, and taking one day at a time. Tell your sisters you love them forever and ever. Tell them they are beautiful. Be thankful for what you have. Get dressed and never give up.

You are a flower picked especially by God. Provide yourself with a purpose to smile every day you wake up and let your vision be a success. Create a life that feels good on the inside. Learn to share your joy with others. Not everyone will understand your journey. Your difficulties come to make you free. Point out what you love about yourself. When you find the courage, that should be your happy moment.

Sistah, remember you are beautiful. Be someone that no one thought you could get to like me. If I could do it, so can you. You have come a long way. You are better, brighter, stronger when sisterhood comes together.

Meditation Scriptures:

- ❖ Romans 3:21-31
- ❖ 1 Corinthians 13

IN THE MIDST OF IT ALL

- ❖ Luke 1:35
- ❖ Matthew 7

Lord, nothing comes before You. Lord, Your peace You give me. You have done marvelous things. Jesus, You are the center of my joy. Bless me now. I pray for change in my circumstances. Lord, I honor You. In Jesus' Name, Amen.

A GODLY WOMAN

Is Led by the Word – Luke 1:38

Is Trustworthy – Proverbs 31:11-12

Is Hardworking – Ruth 2:17

Is Teachable – Esther 2:15

Submits to Her Husband – Ephesians 5:22-23

Speaks with Wisdom – Proverbs 31:16

Produces Good Work – 1 Timothy 2:10

Cares for Her Household – Proverbs 31:27

Practices Self-Control – Titus 2:3

I WON'T BE HER

I want better. God shows you by example how you need to be. God shows you the pattern of the proper foundation for all of your love relationships. When you love someone dearly, you are willing to give freely. Give up some things. It is hard sometimes, but through prayer, you can conquer all. God offered you new life when He laid down His life for you.

The exciting thing is that when you give to God, you really do not lose anything. You want to love others as God loves you. Nothing is more satisfying than serving the Lord, knowing that you are in His will. You want to be able to trust your family and friends and show them that Agape Love.

When you put your trust in God, you put all your weight on Him. You deserve better. You need to live an unstoppable life.

The book of Psalms tells you how you can get better things in life. To know yourself is to love yourself. If you accept who you are, then you can grasp on to bettering yourself.

You need to push yourself. Once you accept your well-being, do not change for anyone. You have to make major decisions in life if you want better. You have to work on yourself. God wants to prosper you. God wants to save you. Make changes in your daily walk of life. There is always room for improvement. Set a goal and work towards it.

IN THE MIDST OF IT ALL

Meditation Scriptures:

- ❖ Psalm 119:72
- ❖ Psalm 37:16-17
- ❖ Matthew 6:19-21
- ❖ Romans 5:8

Lord, I want to be better. I want to live better. I need Your strength. I need Your love. I need Your guidance. I know with You all things are possible. In Jesus' Name, Amen.

THE BEST IS YET TO COME

I used to get discouraged. I felt like the weight was on my shoulders. I felt like the whole world was against me. Sometimes it seemed like a never-ending struggle to keep my life in line. I am here to encourage you that no matter what you are going through or what you have already endured, the best is yet to come. The one thing I learned is that God will not put more on you than you can bear. Just continue to pray and have faith. Always hold on because help is on the way.

There is a blessing coming through just for you. You must realize that no matter what the situation is, God is still in control. Sometimes family and friends try to make you doubt your dreams or what God has spoken. You need to continue pressing your way and not stop every time an obstacle comes.

The glory of the latter shall be greater than the glory of your former house. The greater your storm, the brighter your rainbow will be. Continue to spread joy. Sometimes you struggle from day-to-day trying to keep your head above water. You go through daily routines. Be happy always because you have not seen your best yet, but it is coming.

No matter how young or old you may be, you will have some good and bad days. Just look up and hold on to your faith. The best is on its way.

IN THE MIDST OF IT ALL

Do not stop at the crossroads of life. Do not yell, scream, or throw in the towel. Hold on. There is a master plan to help you get to your destination. There is a brighter day and a better way. Your best is yet to come.

Meditation Scriptures:

- ❖ 1 Corinthians 2:9
- ❖ Luke 5:1-11
- ❖ John 2:1-8
- ❖ James 1:14-15

Lord, I thank You, for I know that through Your Word, better days are coming. I thank You for the gift of love You have given me because I am Your child. In Jesus' Name, Amen.

YOU CAN CHANGE

The most positive thing about life is you have a choice to change. When I was growing up, I had a lot of dreams. I wanted to be the best at everything I put my hand on. Did it happen that way? No.

After leaving high school, I wanted to party, drink, and run the streets. I looked up, and life was passing me by. I was a young mother, not knowing what to do with a child. I was in relationship after relationship, trying to find love. I was always told I would never amount to anything. I had my heart broken many times. I gave all I could and was still heart-broken. Many days I cried, saying, "Things will get better, my life will improve. I will prove folks wrong."

I praise God for my past. It taught me some valuable lessons. My future depended on no one but me. I had to change my mindset and the company I kept. I learned to pray more. I learned to seek God more, and most importantly, I learned not to worry about what people say about you.

Focus on yourself. God made you His own. The love of God leads you to a better understanding. I allowed people to pull me way down. I began to question myself. "If I wait long enough, will my life get better? What are my choices?" I had to let go of regrets and face my fears head-on (Genesis 41:16).

You have the power to change. Being encouraged daily helped me get through the trying times in my life. God is always at work.

IN THE MIDST OF IT ALL

He renewed me. Never let your emotions make you decide. I felt like I could not change, but thank God I did.

Meditation Scriptures:

- ❖ Mark 9:23
- ❖ Psalm 40:17

Lord, I need Your power. Lord, I need Your touch to make it from day-to-day. I depend on You. Lead me to the rock that is higher than I. In Jesus' Name, Amen.

LOVE

Love is patient and kind. You should be mindful of what you say and how you treat others. When you are in love, it should show on your face. I am not speaking about men. I am talking about loving yourself first. Look to Jesus. Let Him be the first in your life (Matthew 6:33).

Can you imagine how great your life would be if you just held on to God? True love begins with the love of God (1 John 48:10). God not only tells you what true love is; He shows you. When He sent Jesus to earth to die for your sins, God did not wait around for you to start living right. He loves you if you are right. He loves you even when you are wrong.

You want to experience the shift of love, true love that God gives you. The Lord's love is amazing. His commandments are true.

Have you experienced heartbreak because you just knew it was for real, only to find out you thought you were in love? That is the worst feeling. Can you imagine God doing this to you? Leaving you all by yourself and not answering your prayers? That would not feel good.

To be reminded by scripture daily helps your daily life.

IN THE MIDST OF IT ALL

Love is one powerful word! Sometimes you find temporary fulfillment in your life because you stopped looking at yourself. You are beautiful and wonderfully made. God knows the real you no matter how you try to hide. He knows you inside and out. He knows your going and your coming. Thank God He loved you long before you knew Him.

God never changes. You change. You try to look and be like someone else. Enjoy loving you. God knows your past, present, and future. There is complete rest in God.

You can be yourself when it comes to Him. He loves you just the way you are.

Where is your heart today?

What is on your heart when you wake up?

What thoughts have you hidden in your heart?

Meditation Scriptures:
- ❖ Romans 13:8
- ❖ Luke 10:27
- ❖ John 3:16
- ❖ 1 Corinthians 13:4-5

IN THE MIDST OF IT ALL

- ❖ 1 Corinthians 16:14
- ❖ Song of Solomon 8:7
- ❖ Proverbs 3:3-4

God, You bring such a gift to me. Wrap Your arms around me. Let me feel Your love today and every day. Above all, show me how to love because it covers a multitude of sins. I should carry love in my heart today and forever. In Jesus' Name, Amen.

JUST WAIT

God has someone incredible for you. You may go through numerous relationships but wait patiently on the Lord. Sometimes you love too hard because you do not want to be alone. When you least expect it, love will find you. You need to hear God's voice and wait on His timing.

Getting to know a person and falling in love is better than rushing a love that will not work. You can be in a relationship for years, but it will not work if you both are pulling in the wrong direction. God wants you to have someone that brings the best out of you – laughter, smiles, and conversation. One day you will sit back and thank God you did not settle, and you waited on God's plan for your life. Always stay humble and guard your heart. When your Boaz comes, you will know he simply adores you with every flaw, and he still cares.

He is a Godsend when he puts God first, knows how to pray, and wants to walk with you in life. He is not afraid to love you. When you are together, you become his best friend, his confidant, the person that holds him down. He is your biggest fan. You will walk hand in hand. Showing you respect is number one in his book. You are his queen. He will spend time with you, and you will not have to beg for his attention. He will bring the beauty out of you that you had hidden on the inside.

IN THE MIDST OF IT ALL

You will know you are worthy of his love. You will have ups and downs, but with God, nothing will fail. When you pray silently, God hears you, and on His time, He will answer. A man after God's own heart will lead you to Christ. A spiritual relationship is ordained by God. Only God can give you the love you are looking for. It is out there. Be patient and wait.

Meditation Scriptures:

- ❖ Psalm 90:12
- ❖ 1 Peter 4:8
- ❖ Ephesians 4:2-3

Thank You, Lord, for giving me blessing after blessing. I pray for patience and strength, knowing that all things are possible if I believe. In Jesus' Name. Amen.

A NEW BEGINNING

Some days my plans were put on hold, and I had to focus on mending my heart. You may never understand the wisdom of God, but you have to trust His will. Sometimes you wonder why you have trapped emotions. You have them because you have ignored or blocked yourself from spiritual healing. You create new challenges and do not give yourself a chance to renew your mind or body to feel free again and move forward towards a better life. When you truly forgive, you will have no emotion from it. There is something about pain that makes you feel like you are struggling. When you overcome being trapped, you will value yourself more and be the best.

Sometimes you do not plan to have things happen in your life. You will fail if you do not succeed.

You have to forget things that are behind you. Do not let your defeats take over you. Your faith is often limited by what you have experienced in the past. Trusting God will make all things new. He can do in your life what you have never seen before. God does not want you to stay where you are.

New beginnings come to those who step out on faith. God wants you to walk by faith and trust Him and see your future through His eyes. God's grace and mercy are new every day. There are chains that keep you from moving forward and set you free from wrong thinking. Imagine spending your life waiting and hoping every day.

Philippians 4:6 says do not be anxious about anything but in everything, by prayer and supplication, make your requests known unto God.

Every day is a new day and a day of thanksgiving. Be thankful for what you have. God stands beside you through your change. New beginnings can be a joy, and they also can be a challenge. Sometimes your path is clear, and sometimes it is rocky.

Why is a fresh start good?

How can you make life better?

What are you grateful for?

You are called to love others God's way:

- ❖ John 13:34-35
- ❖ 1 John 4:8
- ❖ Matthew 5:16
- ❖ Deuteronomy 11:1
- ❖ John 13:34

Love is more than a feeling. You must be more tuned into God and allow Him to teach of His Word that He commands. You must continue to encourage and pray, and God will continue to bless you and the people around you. Find your peace in the midst of it all. Try not to focus on the what if I but focus on what will.

IN THE MIDST OF IT ALL

When you know the all-knowing God, you understand your purpose.

❖ Proverbs 3:5-6
❖ Psalm 46:10

I finally get what my grandmother implanted in me, "When in the midst of it all, God tells us to love and let live." A new beginning has opened. Learn from past mistakes and be an encourager. Teach the ones that have a desire to listen and learn to love.

Your first step is loving yourself; then, you can pour into someone else.

❖ Psalm 138:7
❖ 2 Thessalonians 3:3
❖ Jeremiah 17:7-8

Meditation Scriptures:

❖ Proverbs 11:16
❖ Proverbs 27:12
❖ Proverbs 14:1
❖ Proverbs 31:9
❖ Titus 2:3-5

Thank You, Lord, for a new start. Thank You for watching over my life. Lord, I trust in Your Word. Please help me to move forward every day. In Jesus' Name, Amen.

REFLECTION

As days went by, I began to look at myself in the mirror. I looked at then to how I am feeling now. I had so much anger built up on the inside. I had to turn that frown into a smile. It did not happen overnight. It took me years to find the peace I needed. I kept running back to the same thing I was trying to get rid of. It had a hold on me. I tried over and over, but I still kept running back to it. I was stressed to the max. I tried meditation many days. It worked for a while, but I had to remind myself that I am coming out of this with my hands up. I had to get to know myself and love my inner self.

Sometimes we have so much going on in our lives: anxiety, fear, anger, depression, abuse, negativity, and stress. I had to look at myself and desire change.

Every day got less stressful. I was putting God first, then myself. I began to look at myself daily, wanting to smile again.

I wrote a song, *"Here I am, Lord looking in the mirror, what do I see? Hurt, pain, and disappointment staring back at me."* Then I made up in my mind I am not going through this anymore. I know God has so much in store.

I wanted to be able to see my true beauty. I wanted to be looked at without scars and tears, so I prayed the prayer of release.

IN THE MIDST OF IT ALL

Meditation Scriptures:

- ❖ Matthew 11:25-27
- ❖ Isaiah 10:5-7
- ❖ 2 Corinthians 4:6
- ❖ Job 37:18
- ❖ Proverbs 27:19

Lord, this time I am coming to You with open arms and a get right heart. I want to change my life. I am a sinner saved by grace. Thank You, Lord, for loving me when I did not love myself. In Jesus' Name, Amen.

STRENGTH

You have to be reminded of how strong you really are. You tried to hold on to excess baggage; it did not work. It is time to move on with bettering your life. God will make room for you. If He did it before, He will do it again. Never forget how far you have come.

When you pushed and felt like you were not moving, you were developing strength along the way. When you come to God and are broken, He cleans you up and helps you regain your focus. It is a growing experience. That is where you gain your strength. When you cannot do it on your own, the Lord gets you through. Focus on yourself first. The Bible says, "Blessed are the meek for they shall inherit the earth." Your strength is made perfect in weakness.

There was a woman in the Bible named Deborah. She obeyed and spoke God's Word. She reminds you that no matter how long you have been stuck in a tradition, you can break the chains of life and pull through in this world. Never be afraid. God is greater than your issues. A woman of strength always kneels to give God glory and pray her strength comes within. When you think you cannot go on, you actually can. Ephesians 6 tells us, "Finally be strong in the Lord in His mighty power. Put on the full armor of God so that you can take your stand against the devil's schemes."

Continue to walk hand-in-hand with God. Know the meaning of grace. Be passionate about your accomplishments.

IN THE MIDST OF IT ALL

Meditation Scriptures:

- ❖ Psalm 28:7
- ❖ Deuteronomy 31:6
- ❖ 1 Corinthians 10:13
- ❖ 1 Chronicles 16:11
- ❖ 2 Timothy 1:7

Lord, Your love is amazing. Empower me. Let Your love be that Agape Love. Let my heart be unselfish. In Jesus' Name, Lord, strengthen me. Amen.

MY PAST MADE ME

Many times, you go through life and feel like there is no going forward after this battle. You take life for granted and do things without thinking. Always remember you are stronger than you think you are. God knows your future. You have to understand you are not your downfall. You may screw up sometimes, but you always bounce back. The situation you are in at the moment, good or bad, there is a reason for it. Trust me; it will get better. There is always a light at the end of the tunnel.

You must accept your past mistakes and not allow them to define you. You have to let yourself grow. Do not let your past haunt you. Remember, no matter what you have been through, there is always someone there to pick you up, hold your hand, and whisper everything will be alright. Never be ashamed of your past. The past made you who you are today. You have accomplished so much on this journey. Your past shapes you and prepares you for your future. Never give your past power. You can create your own story and turn it into a testimony to help someone else. Your past does not deserve an explanation. It is over. You have to forgive and make peace with your past faults.

The scripture says, the next time Satan reminds you of your past, remind him of his future (Matthew 25:41).

IN THE MIDST OF IT ALL

Meditation Scriptures:

- ❖ Psalm 103:12-13
- ❖ 1 John 1:9
- ❖ Hebrews 10:17
- ❖ Isaiah 43:25
- ❖ Isaiah 43:18
- ❖ Philippians 3:13-14

Lord, I come humbly asking for my past to stay there and look toward the future. Nobody knew the trouble I had, but You and You released it and made my life new again. Thank You, Lord. In Jesus' Name, Amen.

NEVER LOOK BACK

I was tempted in areas of my life. I knew it would be impossible to follow Jesus and the world at the same time. Turning away from God is dangerous. I was stubborn and wanted to do things my way. I was angry with the whole world for situations I put myself in. I had to learn to live for myself. I had to overcome some obstacles. I had to put self on hold and think about others.

How could I be effective in the will of God? It was time to watch what came out of my mouth. You need to understand that you come to the knowledge of believing when you say you want to grow. You need to be able to show maturity in your walk, especially your talk. You have to set a standard for your life and not fall into others' negativity that will keep you from things in the atmosphere. Be careful not to get in a stagnated situation.

I know you will succeed. I know you will be above in all you ask or think. Instead of hurting others, set an example. There is power in the tongue, and faith will keep you doing right if you trust yourself, humble yourself, pray, be specific, and take no thought for tomorrow.

The Bible says, "Resist the devil, and he will flee." No matter what the situation, it is never bigger than God.

It is time to get up and never look back. Watch what you say and be victorious in your win. Your purpose is not to be afraid. If you believe in your heart, you will know in your heart that no one can change that path you are on.

Meditation Scriptures:

- ❖ Proverbs 13:3
- ❖ Proverbs 21:23
- ❖ James 3:5
- ❖ Philippians 4:4

Lord, teach me in this hour my purpose. Teach me what to say and how to treat others. Instruct me to be a great steward. Thank You, Lord. Prepare me to speak what You will have to say. In Jesus' Name, Amen.

TURN TO JESUS

When life gets rough, where will you turn? Sometimes darkness shatters your life with disappointment, anxiety, suffering, fear, and sin. It also brings you in the midst of hopelessness.

As God was transitioning my life, I found out the love of Christ required me to have a compassionate heart and to turn to Him for the guidance I needed. Trust does not come easy, but you have to have the right mindset. You have to ask yourself can you handle the things of life that come your way. You have to trust Him in simple things. You have to turn to God, not some of the time but all the time.

When you do not trust God, you begin to worry. You can trust God to be faithful. He never changes. He always remains the same. It is so easy to focus on your situations. God deserves sincere thanks. You must trust and praise Him.

There is so much responsibility in becoming a Christian. The day will come when your life will be restored. Turn it over to Jesus and watch how things in your life change for the better. God is going to take what you are going through and turn it into something beautiful. Stop, take time out daily to talk to Jesus. Do not be too busy to talk to Him. Surrender all your worries to God. Your next tears will be tears of joy. Spread the word, prepare, and let your anointing flow. God cares for you.

IN THE MIDST OF IT ALL

Meditation Scripture:

- ❖ Matthew 11:28
- ❖ John 14:1
- ❖ Isaiah 12:2
- ❖ John 4:13-18

God of Abraham, I thank You. I am not perfect. I make mistakes and sometimes mess up, but I turn to You, Jesus, in my weakness. I have a friend in You. I know You are in control. In Jesus' Name, I pray, Amen.

PRAY FOR YOUR CHILDREN

I am still in a state of shock: my only son received 17 years in prison. I raised him to the best of my ability. This was the hurt that almost mentally destroyed me. I cried so many tears, and I was angry. I was blaming God. "How could You do this to me, send my only son away for that many years?"

Through my tears, I realized God put him in a safe place. There is a story to tell and a testimony to be released through him and myself. I had to have the Lord remind me that some things are out of my control, but I can take this situation and help someone else.

Every child needs their mother no matter how old. Continue to keep them covered in prayer. God will provide no matter how far or near they are. Love your children. They are your heartbeat. We all make mistakes, and God forgives.

Make sure your children know you love them unconditionally no matter what they have done. No one is perfect. We all fall and need a hand to get back up again. You cannot let it destroy you. Your past teaches you wisdom every day. Be blessed, thankful, and grateful that you are still alive to talk about it. You matter in this season of life. Speak boldly over your children giving the devil no authority.

Casting all your cares upon Him, for He cares for you. – 1 Peter 5:7

IN THE MIDST OF IT ALL

You should be consistent in your prayers. Sometimes children put you in so much pain and suffering by not listening, and they end up in terrible situations, but in the mix of the mess, God is always present to get you through. God is still God, no matter what happens in life.

We raise our children to the best of our ability, but they stray. I am here to encourage someone, it is not your fault when you raised them right, and they went left. Continue to lift them in prayer. Continue to speak life and hold on to them. One day a change is coming. Your children are important. I was frustrated and worn out because I had to go through things, but I continued to call on the name of Jesus.

The Lord has convinced me over and over how much He loves His children. They are the center of His heart. Children are often overlooked in our society, but they are vital to the community in Jesus' eyes.

Jesus had a heart and compassion for children. You also need the same thing.

Do you love your children and want the best for them? Children are our future—all they owe you is obedience and honor.

If Jesus would have disobeyed His parents even one time, He could not have been perfect and died for our sins, and you could not be saved. This was part of God's great plan. Continue to love on your children. God sees and knows all.

IN THE MIDST OF IT ALL

Meditation Scriptures:

- ❖ Mark 11:23-24
- ❖ 2 Corinthians 4:3-4
- ❖ Matthew 18:18
- ❖ Matthew 9:37-38
- ❖ Ezekiel 36:26-29

Jesus, I come asking You to take away the hurt and the weight of this world. Continue to watch over my children and their children and family. Please help me to understand the things I cannot change. Let me begin to call my children blessed. Bless me through Your Word. In Jesus' Name, Amen.

GOD WILL PROVIDE

God wants you to be content in Him in all situations. God knows everything, so when family does not believe, friends do not believe, when your job is not supplying enough, turn to God and stand. Sometimes you are broken emotionally and financially; your reputation is damaged, and most of all, you are broken because of the ones you thought had your back. You need to continue to keep your faith. You tend to disagree and be skeptical. Expressing yourself through God's will gives you positive quality and assurance. You have to stay faithful to God and the ministry.

You sometimes go into situations with the right intentions, and because of circumstances, you find yourself shackled and bound up and not trusting God. I am so glad we have Jesus that steps right in on time and sets us on the straight and narrow road. Our Father lets us go on our way. Our God is awesome. Having faith in God goes beyond knowing what others believe. You have to hold on. He's your provider, waymaker, counselor, and mind regulator. Sometimes when the enemy has a plan, you must beat him at his own game. The Lord will fight your battles and give you everything you need.

God will bring you out of darkness to the marvelous light. You have to understand God's vision entirely. He will do what is best for His children and deliver you on time.

IN THE MIDST OF IT ALL

The truth is that God can use you to change and bring you closer to walking with Him. You have to trust the process. Know He will not have you lacking anything. He is Jehovah Jireh, your provider – the source of the supply. God promised that He would meet your needs. He understands your physical and spiritual needs. He is a promise keeper. He may not answer your requests as you want, but He will answer them as He told you He would. He never breaks a promise.

Meditation Scriptures:

- ❖ 2 Peter 3:9
- ❖ Isaiah 43:19
- ❖ Ecclesiastes 3:1-6
- ❖ 2 Samuel 7:28

Dear Lord, I do not see it now but will sooner or later. I put my trust in You. I love You with my whole heart, Lord. Bless my house, align me to Your will and to Your way. Shape me, mold me, and make me. I am Your child, and I worship and praise You. In Jesus' Name, Amen.

WHEN THE UNEXPECTED COMES

Throughout our lives, unexpected things happen. Sometimes we are broken in spirit. When this happens, you have to be reminded that all things work out for your good, and even when you think you are okay, something sneaks in and turns your world upside down. When this happens, you tend to focus on the storm.

How do you overcome and bounce back from a bad situation? Do you have faith to trust in God and lean and depend on Him to see you through? You still have to keep your eyes on Jesus and continue to pray for the situation. You have to meditate and keep believing. Sometimes you may get caught in your feelings. You need strength to make it.

Regardless of how you feel, you still have to let God lead you. Do not allow your mind to wander all over the place because God has given you the power to overcome anything with prayer. He sees your circumstance. Life is going to be full of surprises if you keep living. You may not be prepared for the unexpected. Do not worry about anything, but in everything by prayer and supplication with thanksgiving, let your request be known. If you allow your anxieties to control you, you get beat down by life.

God wants your prayer requests. God wants to be present in your life. God wants you to be prayerful in everything. There is no problem too big or too small for God to solve. You have no way of knowing what the future may hold. It will leave you disappointed and drained. Trust God. The power is in prayer. Anytime God leads, restoration follows. God allows encounters, but in the end, you will be restored. God will turn your troubles into triumph. What was once damaged or ruined, God is going to give you double for your trouble when you least expect it. God is coming to your rescue when you think it is the end, but you will go higher. You have to withstand the storms of life.

The unexpected comes in all forms: bills, legal problems, relationships, sickness, jobs, but you must still trust God and the process.

The rainstorm comes into your life, but know the sun will shine. You will gain strength in difficult times. Through this, you can have a divine purpose.

Meditation Scriptures:

- ❖ Luke 1:30-31
- ❖ Luke 2:7
- ❖ 2 Kings 4:17
- ❖ John 16:13

Lord, show me how to get through unexpected circumstances. Free me from anxiety and stress. I know worrying gets me nowhere. Lord, grant me faith and strength and give me peace in my life. In Jesus' Name, Amen.

SUPPORT SYSTEM

During all my trials and tribulations and all the hurts and scars, I was able to lay aside the worries of life and seek God. I have come to encourage whoever reads this that God is not finished with you yet. If things in your life have been going wrong, there is a breakthrough waiting for you. God wants to prosper and elevate you. Meditate on God's Word night and day.

Praise God in the midst of your storm. He will turn things around for you and whomever you are praying for. When stress comes into your life, you may experience anxiety and fear, but God is with you.

You are not alone. Pray that God will calm your heart and help to lead you into a place of calmness. In the midst of it all, God will prepare a table before you in the presence of your enemies. Ask God to intervene on your behalf so you can trust and follow Him. You want to live a peaceful and productive life. Plug into the spiritual realm of Jesus to know you are safe in His arms.

Get connected with some spiritual people that can pour into your spirit and help you discover your life's purpose. We all have backslidden and disconnected from our Lord and Savior, but ask God to mend you, mold you, and sharpen you so that the feeling you once felt is no longer there. Ask Him to instruct you as you learn to glorify Him in the midst of it all.

IN THE MIDST OF IT ALL

Meditation Scriptures:

- ❖ 2 Peter 1:2
- ❖ Romans 5:3-5
- ❖ Proverbs 2:1-11
- ❖ Isaiah 41:10
- ❖ Colossians 4:5

In the name of Jesus, I command every problem I ever had to leave right now. I decree and declare victory over my life. I am blessed and wonderfully made. I walk worthy, and everything I do and touch will be pleasing to God. I give You thanks. I give You praise. Thank You for guiding me through the troubles of life, and without You, there would be no me. I love You. In Jesus' Name, Amen.

JOY WILL COME

The pain you have been feeling cannot compare to the joy that is coming (Romans 8:18).

Sometimes you cry for no apparent reason. There are times that no matter how much you want to stop crying, you cannot. But there is a day that will come when your crying days will be over; Your joy comes from God. It transforms you. No matter how sad you are, the joy is inside of you. You need guidance and encouragement to be stronger, wiser, and closer to God. We are here to lift each other.

When it comes to the things of God, preparation is the key. God is the giver of joy, so you have to smile and make someone's day. Every prayer you pray, there is a period of waiting. God is faithful, and the smile on your face is pleasing to God. Be filled with the joy of the Lord. You must know in your heart that all things work together to those who love Him. Be still and know that He is God.

Your joy is coming. Open your heart and receive it. Do not worry about what is happening around you. Joy comes in the morning. God is your love, your hope, your peace, and you belong to Him. There is a master plan. Be ready to celebrate, laugh, and dance through the power God has given you. When you decide to make Him the center of your joy, God will do the same for you. True joy is a blessing. It is free to us all!!

IN THE MIDST OF IT ALL

You serve a God that has a plan and a purpose for your life. You serve a God that is greater than all your troubles. You serve a God that makes all things possible.

Meditation Scriptures:

- ❖ Romans 15:13
- ❖ James 1:2-3
- ❖ Psalm 47:1
- ❖ 2 Timothy 4:17
- ❖ Romans 8:18

Lord, I thank You for the joy You give. Now, Lord, from here, create a joyful spirit. Grant me more peace and joy to push and press and prepare me for a great work in You. In Jesus' Name, Amen.

ALWAYS REMEMBER

You are strong.

You are beautiful.

You are amazing.

Keep pushing.

Dream big.

Choose happiness.

Have happy thoughts.

Always smile.

Love yourself.

You will make it through this and come out powerful!!

Stay positive!!

Prioritize what's important to you!!

LOVE AND HAPPINESS

Improve your attitude daily. Sometimes being negative is easy. It requires no help. It comes naturally. It takes a willingness to break through the obstacles in your life. Many people want a miracle, but in life, you have to push through. When I shared my testimony with others, I wanted to share that God sees you. God understands you, and mostly He remembers everything you say or do. Stay positive. God has an ultimate plan for your life, even when you feel you do not deserve it.

There is no limit to God's understanding. His word is true. Focus on things that you love. Fall in love with yourself. Self-love is essential. Learn to use more positive words. Be thankful for the things that happen in your life.

Everything will never be perfect. When trying to reach your goals, things fall apart as you try to pursue your dreams. Keep your mind focused. Surround yourself with positive people. Recognize your strength and always believe you can accomplish anything your heart desires.

Every day brings new choices. Make every day count. Your happiness depends on you.

IN THE MIDST OF IT ALL

Meditation Scriptures:

- ❖ John 4:11-12
- ❖ 1 Peter 1:8
- ❖ Psalm 94:19
- ❖ Galatians 5:22-23

Lord, I love You. I trust You. You are my strength, and my heart leaps with praise. In Jesus' Name, Amen.

LOVE STORY

After all I had gone through, after so many sleepless nights and a pillow full of tears, after enormous hurts and shutting myself out from the public, I waited on God to send me the man that was made perfect just for me. When you are in a hurry to find the right man or get married, you need to remember Ruth's story, how she patiently waited on her Boaz to come.

Ask the Lord to prepare you to be a godly wife. We as women are beautiful and need to be cherished. I went through some bumps and bruises, but when my time was ready and I matured, God blessed me with a man of God who knew how to pray and seek God for himself.

At the end of a dark tunnel, there is light. I want to encourage you, do not settle with being with the wrong one. It will cause you to miss the right one. I had to learn about lust and affection and not love and commitment. Then I was angry and frustrated when it did not work. I had to learn how to set boundaries, but first, I had to love myself before I could love someone else.

When God sent me the man of my dreams, he treated me with the utmost respect. He still opens the car door and pulls out the chair before I sit. This was a new journey for me. I loved it.

Better yourself as a woman and watch God move on your behalf. Commit yourself to God and wait, and let love find you. True love never changes. Find your peace and quietness. Fall in love with

God, and God will send a man that will love you exactly how Christ loves the church.

Lord, fill me with Your Holy Spirit. Thank You, Lord, for I know I am not perfect and come short of Your glory. Thank You for my health and strength. Keep me positive in every situation. In Jesus' Name, Amen.

WHERE DO I GO FROM HERE?

In closing, let me tell you, the truth will set you free. Do you really know the Lord? Have you established a personal relationship with Him? Is your desire to be better? He is the one that promises to keep you in perfect peace when your mind stays on Him. When you realize that you are better at helping others and looking back on life, you are amazed when you start walking and talking boldly and change the way you think and act. Find your assignment. Keep your eyes open and focused. Fast and pray. It is time to throw away the old and be who God created you to be. Settle for nothing less than God's best. Through studying the word, God will reveal to you what your purpose is. God wants you to be faithful to His Word.

Where do you go from here?

Search yourself. Salvation is free. Seek God with all your heart. God is doing marvelous works. The choice is yours.

You can stay where you are, or you can choose to move forward and grow. Moving forward requires stepping out of your comfort zone. It sometimes requires not getting it all together on the first try but having faith and continuing to push, leaving the outcome to our Lord and Savior.

You need to listen. You need to wait on God. Love God and worship Him. You are moving in the right direction to a new and fresh experience with God. Stand on the promises, and you will come out feeling better and stronger.

To everything, there is a season and a time to every purpose under the heavens. – Ecclesiastes 3:1

Without God in your life, where would you be?

Since you have changed, what is different about you?

CONCLUSION

Learn to be content whatever the circumstances (Philippians 4:11). Sometimes in life, we are not as strong as we think we are. We lose control, and we have to recharge our life with Christ. We have to collect our thoughts and position ourselves to be more focused and motivated daily.

You have to remember that no matter how long you are in a situation, God is in the midst of it all. Even amid difficulty, you can find peace in a storm. I can sit for hours and watch and listen to the sea, the water hitting against the rocks. It is beautiful, calm, and peaceful. That is my happiness. No matter how great the storm, God does precious things in our lives even when we think it is turned upside down.

Circumstances can leave us feeling empty and dry in spirit, but God gives us grace in our minds and our lives. God will make a way. Prayer changes things. You have to drop to your knees and pray for a change. You have to say to your inner self, "It is my turn to be in charge, to be happy, and let my light shine." You are responsible for your happiness. You have to chase your dreams. Opportunities are waiting. You have to stop doubting yourself. Develop and maintain a relationship with God. Ask God for a supernatural breakthrough that will bring forth everything you need. Ask God to make a way. Pray that God will continue to show His power towards you.

IN THE MIDST OF IT ALL

When you come out of the storm, you will not feel like the same person that walked into the storm. You will feel like you have overcome. Your path will be much clearer. Prepare yourself to be prosperous. Do not allow fear to stop you.

And Jesus looking upon them saying, with man it is impossible, but not with God, for with God all things are possible. – Mark 10:27